Isandro

hidden journals volume 1

Elle Klass

*Award winning author
of mystery and suspense*

Copyright © 2019 by Books by Elle, Inc.
225 College Dr. Orange Park, Fl 32065
ISBN: 978-1951017002

Cover art created by TL Katt
Editor Dawn Lewis Bookmarks Editing
Website: elleklass.weebly.com

Author's Disclaimer

This book is entirely fictional. Any characters or events are purely figments of the author's imagination. The city of St. Augustine isn't fictional and is in northern Florida. Many of the businesses and locations mentioned in the book can be found there. No part of this publication may be reproduced, transmitted or redistributed either in its entirety or in part without the author's express written consent.

Other books by Elle

The Bloodseekers: St. Augustine Novellas
The Vampires Next Door Book 1
The Monster Upstairs Book 2
The Ghost Within Book 3

hidden journals
Isandro vol. 1
Alarico vol. 2

Zombie Girl
Premonition Book 1
Infection Book 2
Retribution Book 3

Baby Girl
In the Beginning Volume 1
Moonlighting in Paris Volume 2
City by the Bay Volume 3
Bite the Big Apple Volume 4
Caribbean Heat Volume 5
Return to the Bay Volume 6
Prison of the Past Volume 7
Baby Girl Box Set - Volumes 1-4

prologue

The world peaceful and the magic balanced, the Slayers moved on with their lives. They finished high school, went to college, and started careers. By thirty they realized they weren't aging. People were beginning to notice. It was time to leave their present lives. Mandy and the wolves went to Wolf Manor and she started an ecommerce store selling herbal remedies that she spelled with healing magic. Vicky traveled the world working as a freelance photographer and journalist. Opal and Rylan settled in his home country of Spain, in the mountains, where she took an interest in antiques. Lacey worked her way up in the fashion design world, started her own line, and designed on the move. Adrian wrote code and designed video games from home. Rodham and Alison started an online bookstore. It was her idea. The plan was to have a child when the business got off the ground but that didn't happen; maybe fertility was impossible with their immortal bodies. They stayed hidden and kept themselves out of the public eye, but that grew old.

After Opal's parents' deaths they settled into her home in St. Augustine. With Opal's interest in antiques, Alison's in literature they opened an antique store -- Relics in historical St. Augustine -- and they blended into the mystery and paranormal shroud of the city.

St. Augustine had grown, but the historic area was still cryptic and filled with the same legends of the past as if it was molded in time. Alison was never able to remove the spell on Alistair and invited him to live with them. The others were a bit unnerved by someone they couldn't see living with them, and maybe a boggart was a dangerous entity to have around. It turned out his curious nature discovered the secrets of the house. They were hidden in the walls and beneath the floor boards. This is one of the hidden journals he found.

chapter 1

"In here," I whispered, careful my mother didn't hear. I pushed against the heavy wooden door engraved with intricate curves and grooves. The sweet, earthy scent of my father's cigars moved through my nostrils and I inhaled deeply. I always loved the smell and it made me feel safe.

Thick tufts of chestnut hair bounced as Arthur scooted into the room.

"Where is it?" asked Lawrence, his blue eyes searched the large room, studying the walls of leather-bound books and the thick cypress desk.

I swished my mouth to the side in thought. "It was over there yesterday, but I know he hides it."

Arthur leaned his back against a bookcase. "I think you're bluffing."

"No, no it was here," I pleaded. Arthur and Lawrence had never really been my friends. They spent their days bullying and harassing me. When I spotted the silver sword with the orange stone in its handle I thought maybe they'd accept me, stop pestering me.

I pulled out the top drawer of the desk in search of a clue, anything to tell me where the sword was. My father spent a lot of time at his desk when home. Something had to be here. When I found nothing I pushed the drawer back in, lowered myself, and studied the underside.

"It's not here," Lawrence stated mockingly. "Let's get out of here."

Arthur grabbed the shelf behind his neck and curled his fingers beneath it. A clink followed by clunking and grinding stemmed from the bookcase behind him. His eyes widened. "I... I think I did that. There was a flaw in the wood and I pushed it."

We stared as the grinding continued and the wall behind Arthur opened, slowly. Our eyes grew wide when it came to a stop, revealing a hidden corridor.

Lawrence shifted uncomfortably, running a hand through his ginger hair. "A secret room."

I gulped. I didn't know it was there. This was my father's study; even my mom never entered. I'd surely get a lashing if my father knew I was here. I stalked towards it, my heart beating quick and breaths shortened.

The corridor was dark, only the sun's rays from the window of the study offered any light. The floor was wooden, the same as the house. Stone -- one stacked on the other -- made up the walls.

Arthur joined me and stared into the hidden area. Our feet at the doorway. "What do you think is in there?"

"I... I... don't know," I answered.

"I dare you to go inside." Lawrence pushed me from behind and I nearly stumbled into the dark area.

"Isandro!" my father called. Panic hit me in the gut.

I turned on my heel. "We need to close this now or we'll all be in trouble."

"How?" asked Arthur with a shaky voice.

My father was a large, muscular man who was steadfast and firm. Not a person anyone messed with. "Find the flaw and push it or pull it." Anxiety roiled inside me. My father's heavy steps echoed in my ears. It was all I could hear.

Arthur's hands fumbled along the bookcase, searching for whatever triggered the door to open. I joined him frantically searching.

"I got it," Arthur said in a loud whisper. My father's footsteps closer. He pushed against it. The creaking started and then we shot out of the way as the door closed.

"What are you doing in here?" asked my father from the doorway. He searched our faces with a stern eye that shifted from one of us to the next. His jaw straight, which meant nothing good.

The wall only closed into place seconds before he appeared in the doorway. *Does he know? Did he hear it?* I swallowed hard, fear sinking into my gut. *Think, think*, I urged myself. If I didn't come up with something quick I'd be in for more than a lashing. Then I spotted the carved boat I'd made my father. It sat on the corner of his desk. I ran to it and grabbed it, "I wanted to show them this."

The tension in the room built up over an extra-long moment then my father's lips curled in a smile. My heart and guts righted themselves. "Now they've seen it. Time for the boys to go home. Isandro, you have studies to catch up on."

We nodded in unison and released the breaths we were all holding. My father didn't appear to notice. I walked them outside.

"That was better than a sword. Everyone has one of those, but nobody else has a secret room in their house," Lawrence said with bright eyes filled with curiosity.

"We have to come back, explore it," stated Arthur as if he had nerves of the toughest metal. The scare over, he was ready for another rush.

I shook my head. "No, we can't do that. Today was close, next time we get caught and I don't want a lash from my father."

Lawrence stepped forward and stood within a few inches of me. "You say that now but you'll get curious and when you do we're sending you in to explore." His words lingered in the air between us almost as if they were a threat.

I gulped and shifted, trying not to let him feel my fear. Lawrence was two years my senior and stood a full foot taller. I backed away then turned and ran up the front steps to the porch. Without looking back, I scrambled inside the house and to my room. I was in such a hurry I didn't look where I was going and ran smack into my father.

"I'm sorry, Papa," I stated, adjusting myself and studying my shoes to avoid meeting his eyes.

My father lifted my chin and narrowed his deep brown eyes as he stared into mine. "Were they impressed with the boat?" I heard the undertones of suspicion in his voice.

"Yes, Papa," I said, unable to hide the anxiety in my voice.

"Have they threatened you?"

"No, Papa." Guilt riddled me. I shouldn't have been snooping to try and impress Arthur and Lawrence.

My father wrapped a thick arm around my shoulder and squeezed. "You would tell me if they did?"

I nodded. My father knew I was lying. I felt the tension in his arm and the pressure of his hand squeezing my shoulder.

"Nods are not words. What do you say?"

"Yes, Papa. I would tell you." I'd never lied to my father, yet here I was, lying.

"To your studies," my father said and released his grip, dropping his arm.

I couldn't concentrate on my studies. The study and my father's words replayed in my head. I didn't ever want to see the room again, but that was the least of my problems. At school I had to face Arthur and Lawrence. They were older and larger. My mind worked out an avoidance plan. If I stayed in the school house helping the teacher I wouldn't have to go outside and face them. After school I'd move through the trees, hiding. It would take longer to get home but was worth the effort.

My mouth parched from worry I slipped to the stairs then stopped when I heard my mother speak my name. Curious, I stepped away from the stairs and drew closer to their room.

"He's nearly twelve. What is an extra few weeks?" said my father in a tone I recognized as the one he used when he laid down the law.

"Not yet. He's not ready." My mother scowled.

My father cleared his throat. "How do you know? I say he is. It's time."

Footsteps moved across the wooden floor and I stepped backwards into the guest room, keeping my head at the doorway to listen. When they came out I'd simply pull my head in like a turtle.

"Isandro shows no signs. It doesn't fall to all offspring, one sibling may have it while another does not," my mother's words sharp enough to cut through metal.

"I won't push this yet, but soon," my father said, heavy footsteps paced towards the door then stopped. "You saw what happened when he was born. Don't blind yourself now. I can find him a teacher other than his mother." The door creaked open.

I drew my head inside the room as my father pushed the door open. My back against the wall and brain a swirl of confusion. They were talking about me.

What do I need to be ready for? What don't I show signs of?

chapter 2

Since the day I found the hidden room in the study I'd run past it. I wanted no part of it, yet was curious. *Was the sword in the room? Is that where he kept it?*

Isandro, whispered a voice. *Isandro,* it came again, high-pitched like a girl and so quiet it was barely audible. I rushed to the entryway and twisted in a circle, searching for who was calling me.

"Who's there?" I asked the air.

Isandro, come to the secret door.

"No!" I ran to the front door and thrust it open, moist air hitting my face. My mind was undoubtedly playing tricks on me. It was guilt eating at me for lying to my father.

My mind a-flutter, I couldn't concentrate. The voice spoke my name over and over, repeating in my head. I lifted my eyes from my paper and glanced at the other students and studied the teacher. No one else heard it. The voice in my head grew stronger throughout the day. *Isandro, I'm lonely. Isandro, come through the door and play with me.*

When the bell let out, I rushed into the woods, falling against a tree, cupping my hands over my face. "Go away!"

"Who are you talking to?" asked the voice of an angel.

I lifted my head to see Clara's shining blue eyes filled with concern. Her golden locks bounced against her shoulders as she moved closer to me.

"No one. I... uh," I stumbled over my words, embarrassed.

"Oh," one word, not even really a word, but I heard the unmistakable inquisitive tone. "Why don't we walk together?" she suggested, holding her book pouch against her chest.

I didn't hesitate. My heart longed for her. We'd never spoken, but inside I'd always loved her. "OK." I picked my book pouch from the ground. She held out her hand for me. I accepted and a slight buzz tingled through my body from my fingers to my toes. We let go and she rubbed her hand but didn't say a word, neither did I. It was strange, but maybe a buildup of static. I slid the bag over my shoulder.

The next few days we walked home together through the trees. The breeze from Matanzas Bay on our backs. Her blonde hair and light complexion made her blue eyes vibrant.

Clara pulled a blue hydrangea from a bush and tickled my cheek. "Soft, aren't they? I love these." She twirled, her long skirt flowing as it wrapped her legs.

They were beautiful and delicate like her. I picked another and tucked it behind her ear. "That's better."

She smiled and giggled then leaned closer to me. Her face so close I smelled her sweet scent. It lured me like magic. "Thank you." Her soft lips met my cheek, melting me inside.

Emotions and feelings I'd never felt before rose to the surface. This girl was special. She was more than a friend. I glanced into her blue eyes and took her hand in mine, warmth and electricity buzzed between us but we didn't let go.

Huguenot cemetery on one side and the glassy water of Matanzas Bay on the other, Clara stopped. She turned her head and peered over the cement wall at the graves. Many of them non-Catholics who'd perished from yellow fever in the early to mid-1800s.

"Do you really think it's haunted?" she asked, her eyebrows poised in an inquisitive V.

I shrugged. I didn't really think ghosts existed, yet was perplexed at the voice that spoke... only to me. "I guess that depends on whether you believe in ghosts." It was a safe answer. A month ago I would have said no, but now I wasn't so sure that I wasn't being haunted by something.

She glanced into my eyes. "I think it's possible," she said with confidence as if she knew something about the afterlife.

I grabbed for her hand and she accepted. We strolled hand in hand then cut through a small patch of woods. We sat beneath a tall tree. Rays of sun filtered through the leaves and shone against her flaxen blonde hair.

"Two little lovers," said an all too familiar voice. One I tried hard to avoid since the day in my father's study -- Lawrence.

I shifted my eyes from Clara to Lawrence. He stood with the sun to his back staring at us. *How long had he been following?* "Hi, Lawrence," I said, keeping my voice steady.

He sauntered towards us then stopped, leaning his back against a tree. "We should come over again, soon."

Clara glanced from me to him and, as if caught in that momen my nerve endings were on edge, she said, "Go away, Lawrence. You're no good."

He pushed off the tree and plucked a flower then stalked towards her, leaned down and pulled her hair back, sliding the flower behind her ear. "Be careful who you choose to spend time with." He walked off, leaving us both questioning the intentions of that moment.

She plucked the flower from behind her ear and tossed it to the ground. "Don't worry about him. I'll see you tomorrow," Clara said as she rose from her spot and scampered away.

That night the voice woke me from my sleep. *Isandro, come.* Its soothing nature coaxed me out of bed. I slid my hand along the banister as I crept down the stairs, avoiding the creaks. I didn't want to know who was calling. Was it a ghost? I wanted the voice to go away back where it came from. Yet I found myself outside my father's study, my hand pressed against the door.

Isandro, it called. The voice didn't whisper through the air but went straight into my head. My imagination, yet I couldn't turn away and run back up the steps like I wanted. Like I knew I should. If my father caught me, I'd get a licking.

My body, moving against the better judgement of my mind, pushed the door. I stood in the doorway staring into my father's office. The voice called again, coaxing me inside. "Who are you?" I asked, pressing my ear against the secret door.

Rabina, she called but the words never lingered in the air. The words, her calls for me, went directly to my head. *Open the door.*

Without thinking, or even remembering, I found myself staring at the heavy door as it slid open, darkness behind it. I lit a candle from my father's desk and stood at the entrance, debating, but it wasn't that I really had a choice. The voice compelled me, forced me to move into the darkness of the tunnel.

I stepped cautiously, using the light to guide me. "Rabina?" I called. Candlelight bounced off the walls and ceiling, revealing the pattern of the stone.

Closer, Isandro.

The darkness swallowed me except the tiny flame that moved with each of my steps. A musky odor assaulted my nose the further into the tunnel I went. I was so far into the tunnel I couldn't see my father's office anymore. I felt stupid and scared. I was following a voice in my head into my father's secret room that turned out to be a tunnel with an abrupt ending.

I felt along the wall, holding my flame against it. The stones were sealed. Trepidation filled me then and I turned on my heel but I couldn't move back to the safety of my father's study. Instead I held the candle staring at the stone wall. It was a dead end. There was nowhere else to go.

Isandro, it called, much louder this time. I took another step closer to the wall, my face only centimeters from it. I swallowed, shivers ran the length of my spine. Light flickered against the grooves in the rock wall. I rested my free hand against it.

A bolt of heat shot through me and into the brick. I dropped my hand, hitting the corner of a jagged stone it caught the side of my hand, causing a laceration. I lifted it to my mouth and sucked.

Creaks and moans churned from the wall as if a pulley system made of chains were opening something. To my left, the bricks grumbled as they slid open. I gasped and my feet carried me over the threshold to the other side.

It wasn't a choice. The force that coerced me into the secret room, that wouldn't let me leave now, made me step into the area. The musky smell grew ten times more repugnant, causing my nose to wrinkle in disgust. It smelled as though a cast of people had died.

The flame sparked and grew when a blast of chilly air hit it. Staring at me through the darkness was a pair of shining eyes.

chapter 3

My eyes grew wide as the ghostly eyes moved closer, shining at me through the darkness. I wanted nothing more than to run.

Isandro, you don't need to fear me. The voice cut through my skull. My mouth dried from fear and I gathered my spit and swallowed hard.

"Rabina?" I asked.

"Yes." She responded in actual words that sliced the air between us.

"I..." My breathing sped up as I struggled to get the words out. She stood close enough I saw her in full. Long, dark, straight hair fell against her chest and her shining eyes I now saw. They were blacker than her raven hair. She was beautiful and real -- alive.

I felt intimidated in her presence as if I shouldn't be glancing upon her beauty. Anything normal I should have felt or said didn't come to me and my words dissipated.

She couldn't have been older than me, was possibly younger. "You saved me." She grabbed my hands before I could pull them back. Her skin felt cool. But probably mine did too as it was chilly where we stood.

"We should get you out of here." It made sense. She couldn't live down here. There was no food, no sun, nothing but an awful stench and the absence of light.

Her full, heart-shaped lips formed a smile. "No, I can't leave here. I only wanted you to join me. I am lonely."

A cool finger brushed against my cut. It wasn't nearly as bad as I'd originally thought. She dropped my hands and turned around as if ashamed.

"What's wrong?"

Her elbows at waist level, she lifted her hands to her face. "Nothing. It's been a long time since I've had someone to talk to."

I touched her shoulder and she spun around, dropping her hands to her sides. "Why are you here?" The question playing on my lips finally dropped.

She slid her tongue across her lips as if appreciating every bite of a good meal. Her black eyes peering into my soul. "I have a disease." She dropped her eye. "I'm allergic to daylight and so I spend my days here."

I couldn't imagine what that would be like. "Then I will come see you again."

"I would like that." She lifted her eyes and met mine. Our gazes froze.

"I have to go now." I stepped back into the corridor. I'd been down there too long already. I was a bit surprised when the constraining force didn't stop me from leaving as if I was meant to meet her. That moment was somehow my destiny. "Do you need anything?" I asked before closing the door.

She shook her head.

"I'll return then, as soon as I can." I pushed the jutted stone and the door returned. Chained pulleys that I hadn't noted on the other side of the wall clinked as it fell into place.

An eerie feeling advanced through me and I practically ran through the corridor into my father's office, quickly shutting the door. It wasn't Rabina that put the fear into me but what my father would do if he caught me.

I took a moment and rested against the wall, catching my breath, then pushed forward and padded to the door, attempting to be church mouse quiet so he wouldn't hear me. The whole idea of sneaking up the stairs because I'd be too loud was preposterous since the loud clanking of the door hadn't woken him.

Once I reached the top of the stairs I slipped into my room and pulled the covers tight to my chin. *Would I visit her again?* Every part of my senses and intuition screamed and begged for me to never return.

chapter 4

The sun spilled through the curtains, announcing morning's return. I blinked my eyes a few times, adjusting to the bright light. A dull anxiety resting in my gut. Rabina's pale skin framed with black hair and eyes took residence within the folds of my brain. *Had I really snuck into my father's office, ran through the corridor and met her? Was she real at all?* It couldn't be. I wasn't brave enough to go against my father. He was a mighty man and didn't tolerate disobedience and Rabina was too beautiful to be anything other than a dream.

It was preposterous; people don't live in the ground. *What would she eat? How would she bathe or go to school?* Shaking my head and scattering the all too real image of Rabina from my mind, I readied myself for school and grabbed my satchel. Slipping it over my shoulder, I plodded down the steps to the kitchen for breakfast.

My parents didn't give me the evil eye or say anything about my sneaking into my father's office. It was ridiculous because they would have heard the secret door open since it clanked and moaned.

"Drink your milk," my mother ordered as I finished my bowl of grits, took a sip and placed the glass back on the table mostly full.

"Yes, Mom." I picked the glass back up and swallowed the rest of my milk.

I couldn't concentrate on studies in class, my mind returning to the dark hall and Rabina. "You're far away," came a sweet voice.

I turned to see Clara's sparkling blue eyes and near-flawless oval face. "I didn't sleep well."

She leaned in and whispered in my ear, "Meet me tonight in the cemetery."

I opened my mouth to speak but she was already gone. I couldn't imagine any reason she'd want to meet in a cemetery at night. The spirits of the dead crawled over my skin as I considered whether I should.

When darkness fell and my parents were soundly asleep I slunk down the stairs, again avoiding the creaky steps, and slipped out the door. Meeting Clara at night was preposterous, yet edgy. If I was caught I wouldn't be able to sit for a month.

Clara hadn't been specific about which cemetery but I had a good idea the one she meant. The one we passed on our walks home -- Huguenot. The one haunted by the judge whose golden teeth were stolen, and the victims of a yellow fever outbreak. Hair prickled over my arms as shadowy figures edged into my side vision with the ghostly thoughts.

When I turned my head I was alone, reminding myself that ghosts didn't really exist. Rabina was human. I even forced a chuckle to lighten my mood and wash away the tension, but it didn't really work. Matanzas Bay's breeze pushed against me, sweeping my hair over my forehead. Running a hand over the top of my head I forced the hair back into place and out of my eyes.

The curves of the sign moved upward into an arch, a circle enclosed a triangle, beneath were the words Huguenot Cemetery. My father once said the circle-triangle symbol was used because the people buried there weren't Catholic and so were considered pagan or satanic. It made me wonder if that's why there were so many ghost stories circling this particular cemetery. The spirits were unsettled...

It was difficult to live in a city that bounded with hauntings and ghost sightings even though I'd always thought them silly... still it was what horror was made of. A warm hand touched mine and a tingle buzzed through my extremities. Out of shock, and spooked from my own ruminations about graves spread out before my eyes, I jumped.

Clara chuckled. "It's me."

All my restless thoughts evaporated when I faced her. Clara was irresistible to me. I admitted to myself I had a crush on her since we first met in school. There was something about her beyond her obvious beauty and kind personality that attracted me. One day, maybe she would be mine and so I'd followed my twelve-year-old heart.

The Matanzas breeze steady in the night carried her curls over her cheeks then dropped them in place. Her natural blush lips curled into a smile as our eyes met.

I tented my hands for her to crawl over the cement fence of the cemetery so she wouldn't get a rip or snag in her jeans. She rested on the curved top before jumping to the ground. A hand on her slightly jutted hip, she cleared her throat.

I sucked in a deep breath and exhaled as I lifted myself over the short cement wall.

She giggled. "Not scared are you?"

It wasn't so much fear as it was an intense gut feeling tonight wasn't going to go well. Headstones of all shapes and sizes; some crosses, others appeared like above ground tombs walling us in, but my mind forgot all about them and my quirky gut as it rested on Clara.

She took my hands in hers. A shock buzzed through my fingers and up both my arms.

"Do you feel that?" she asked.

I nodded but lacked any words. A chill ran up my spine as an icy breeze blew over us. The dim light of the crescent moon gave this resting place of the dead an extra-spooky feel and I swore I heard spirits chattering. *You don't even believe in ghosts,* I reminded myself unconvincingly.

Inside the cement and wrought iron fencing, trees enclosed the graves like protectors. Their leaves rose from the dirt and tumbled in the air surrounding us like we were standing in the center of a water spout on land. I let go of one of her hands and grabbed a leaf that sailed past me. The breeze caught it then pushed it across a pointed headstone. All the other leaves dropped then.

An impish smile played against her lips. "Take my hand again."

With a questioning raise of an eyebrow I rested my hand in hers. The leaves growing from the branches above us rustled. I let go and they suddenly stopped as if the breeze moved on -- except there was no breeze. The air was still for the moment.

Both brows lowered now, I didn't understand what was happening or what exactly she was trying to show me. She held her hands, open palmed, in front of her chest and moved them towards her. From the ground rose a small bouquet of wildflowers from a grave beside us.

I watched. My mouth dropped open as the bouquet suddenly fell to my feet. I stuttered as the words tried to form, "Did... you. What...?"

She grabbed my hands again. "We, I'm stronger with you."

"What are you talking about?" The words finally made their way out.

"Since I was little, I feel energy sometimes when people touch me, but when you took my hand the other day I felt a surge pulse through me that stayed until we let go. After then things started moving around me when I would think about them. Little things like my pencil at school or a page in a book would flip itself, but with you we made the leaves swirl." Her words were so confident I couldn't tell her all that was impossible.

People don't control such things with their minds. At the same time the buzz of energy between us was real, a buildup of static that maybe forced things in its field to move. I convinced myself in the moment that that was it. Of course, it was the only logical conclusion my mind could find. "I think we should go home before we are caught."

"Isandro, you are always so careful but I think there is something inside us -- magic." Her blue eyes lit up.

"Shh!" was my automatic response as if I had to quiet her from saying more. "That's enough." It wasn't only her words and crazy talk from the moment we entered the cemetery, I felt something inside as if someone was trying to reach me from beyond the grave. Chills spiked up and down my arms.

"What are the lovebirds doing out here? A cemetery isn't the proper place for a date." I heard the words before I spotted Lawrence's face.

Turning on my heel, he stood a few feet from us, arms folded over his chest and Arthur at his side. I hoped they hadn't been there long and heard Clara's silly talk or, worse, seen the leaves and bouquet that moved on their own. "We're leaving," I said, grabbing Clara's hand to walk her home.

The place was eerie enough without adding trouble to the mix. The mischievous glint in Lawrence's eyes gave me an overwhelming urge to flee.

The rustle of leaves and footsteps behind us told me they'd split up and were moving closer to us. "No you're not." Lawrence moved in front of us, Arthur I felt on my backside. Between the gravestones and trees we might be able to split up and get away.

Clara squeezed my hand and a group of leaves rose and swept over Lawrence's face, blinding him for a second. "Now, Isandro," she whispered loudly as she pulled my arm, her feet swiftly hitting the ground with each step as I hurried to keep pace with her.

The ground rumbled beneath our feet. As it rose my foot caught on a root and I tripped taking Clara with me. Losing our grip on each other to keep our faces from planting in the ground. A strong wind swept over us as we attempted to scurry to our feet. Its force knocked us down, stopping our efforts. Lawrence stood above us, his eyes in slits and ginger hair with not a strand out of place as if the wind didn't touch him.

Emotions, not words, shot through me and I knew he wanted me for my father's sword. It had something he needed, not only him. Having possession of it would put him in good standing with someone. Arthur joined his side, his brown hair lying flat against his head.

Arthur raised his hand and a dirt wall closed Clara and me in. She grabbed my hand once again. Lawrence cocked his head to the side, bones cracking as he did so. The wind gyrated above the circle of dirt, boxing us in.

My pulse quickened as terror worked its way through my veins. Clara squeezed my hand so tight it hurt, and the gravestones behind Lawrence and Arthur wiggled then rose from the ground. Her expression was steady and I realized she was doing it -- making the gravestones move.

I swallowed hard and concentrated on them to offer her everything I had in me. She raised her free hand and pulled it towards her. The stones hurtled forward, aimed at Lawrence and Arthur.

Lawrence raised an arm and forced the wind circling us to blow the stones backwards. They dropped and broke in pieces above their respective graves. I gasped, unable to believe what was happening. It was a dream -- a nightmare.

"We know what Clara can do, but what about you?" Lawrence stated, kicking the dirt in front of his foot. It carried on a breeze and landed in our faces.

Me? I couldn't do anything. Swells of greed and white hot anger seeded in my head but they weren't my feelings. All I felt was confusion. I wrapped those foreign emotions and pushed them out. I didn't want to feel them. I focused my eyes on Arthur and he fell to his knees clutching his gut.

He raised his head, his dark eyes staring into mine. "Stop," he seethed.

Surprised at his words, I let the malicious emotions dissipate into the night and he rose to his feet.

Lawrence clapped his hands. "Nice, really nice. The children of Slayers are witches themselves."

Witches? Is that what was happening? A battle between witches and what is a Slayer? I thought, answering my own question.

A ball of light caught the boys from behind and they dropped to the ground. A male voice in my head said *Run, go home.* Normally that was something I would have questioned but not in that moment. Lawrence and Arthur incapacitated, I grabbed Clara's hand, welcoming the buzz between us. We scrambled to our feet and sprinted. This wasn't the moment to question the strange events of the night.

Our strides faster than I ever imagined, we ran through the graveyard, stopping and catching our breath in the woods outside Clara's home. A bolt of lightning hit earth a few feet from us. There hadn't been a cloud in the sky. My eyes glanced upwards, taking in the twinkling stars. Rain moved in quickly at times but there was no hint of a storm.

I felt Clara take a step back. Dropping my eyes, a man, hair black as the night air around him and dark eyes, stood where the lightning had hit as if it had dropped him off.

chapter 5

The night only grew stranger as Clara and I moved closer together, our feet in running stances.

"Don't be alarmed," the man said as he stepped towards us. His long, cream suit jacket and slacks seemed really out of place, or more out of the wrong era. "Both of you have come of age and you're learning what you are. You need to prepare to take your place in the battle."

Nerves and uncertainty crawled through Clara. I wasn't positive how I knew, I simply did. "We have magic." The words tumbled from her mouth as if at first she didn't believe them until they were completely out.

He nodded. "Light witches. Those boys are witches coming of age and into their powers too but they will use theirs to harm your kind. They are night witches." The wind pushed the coat tails of his jacket over the sides of his legs and over his face. He pushed the hair back, revealing his dark, intense eyes.

This was getting too silly and out of hand as I listened to his words and his offer to help us learn to use our powers. I didn't have any powers and whatever happened at the cemetery was a fluke, the wind, maybe an unsettled ghost. *Was it stranger to believe in spirits than it was in magic?*

"I need to get home," I stated. "My parents will wonder where I am." I matched his grim expression with one of my own.

He held his palm up and balanced a growing light. My eyes widened as the white light doubled then tripled in size and with a swish from his other hand over the light it was gone. "I will teach you to do that. Go home now and meet me here tomorrow."

As I walked, the events of the night played through my brain. I couldn't wrap my head around what I'd seen. It was all impossible. The only thing I knew for sure was that I wasn't meeting him anywhere! I pushed the backdoor of my house open and crept through the kitchen careful not to wake my parents then, avoiding the creaky steps, went to my room.

The next day I didn't meet the man or witch or whatever he was. It seemed like a dream but I knew deep down it was real. Instead I waited for my parents to leave. They were attending a party and wouldn't return for many hours. I slipped into my father's office and with a lantern made my way into the bricked secret tunnel, coming to the end I spotted the stone that stood out further than the others.

The tunnel was still creepy and the strange odor became more robust, and the sweet scent of my father's cigars grew weaker until it vanished from the air completely. Everything was just as I remembered it. It wasn't a dream. To further confirm my thoughts I pushed the stone down and heard the clack and crank as the door opened to my side.

"You came back," said a sweet voice -- Rabina.

The strong odor hit my nostrils again, forcing me to consider why had I come back?. *What was I doing? Was I checking to see if she was real? Maybe there was something horribly wrong with me.* Breathing from my mouth to avoid the smell I held the lantern level with my head. She stepped backwards out of the light. I moved forward wanting to see again her beauty. Raven hair offsetting her pale skin and dark eyes that were windows of the soul.

"You shouldn't see me," she dropped her head as I stepped closer.

I pressed a hand beneath her chin and lifted it. "Why?" Any anxiety I felt drifted away. I was supposed to be here.

"My eyes are sensitive to the light." She forced her chin down against my hand, not allowing me to see her face.

The lantern was much brighter than the candle had been, I reasoned. "My parents are gone, come with me upstairs. We have food," I offered. It was the very least I could do.

She stepped backwards, pressing her back against the wall as if frightened. "I shouldn't."

I brushed my free hand against one of hers, feeling the unnatural coolness of it. "It's OK. Trust me."

Her head still bowed, she allowed me to take her hand. She wrapped her fingers around mine as if attempting to suck in the heat, and I guided her out of the room then into the stone corridor and into my father's study.

I set the lantern on the table and lowered the amount of light, not flipping any light switches as we went. Her head didn't move above her chest. In the dim light I spotted points on the sides of her head raised through her straight hair. She appeared different than she had the other night in the darkness when she was more than willing to allow me to see her face. *What had changed?*

In the kitchen I left her at the table and grabbed a plate I'd made for her from dinner, placing it on the table before her. I expected she'd quickly devour it, instead she stared at it.

"Eat, you need real food."

She grazed over the broccoli with a nail tip. Her fingers long and slender, almost claw-like stepped to the steak. Without picking up a utensil she grabbed the steak whole and brought it to her mouth.

"I hope it's not too rare," I said with uncertainty. My parents both liked it that way so that's how Mom cooked it.

She stuffed the end of the steak into her mouth. Her hair moved up and down as she chewed. One bite led to another. She didn't say another word until she'd devoured every bite. "Thank you." She licked the red juice from her fingers, savoring the richness.

I pushed a strand of her straight dark hair towards her ear. It appeared much thinner in the dim light of the kitchen then it had in the dark tunnel room. She tilted her head away from my finger as I tucked the strand behind her ear.

Her pointed ear. I sucked in a breath from shock then countered with a fake cough to avoid making her nervous. She'd said she had a disease. The pointed ears no doubt had to be part of that. People had rounded ears.

She quickly pushed the strand from behind her ear so it fell against her cheek once again. More curious than ever, I attempted to raise her chin. "I'm not going to hurt you. I just want to see you."

She swallowed hard and I felt her cringe with tension as I guided her chin upright. I almost jumped out of my chair, aghast, when her dark eyes, absent of white, met mine. She was the same girl I'd seen the other night, only then I saw what I wanted to see. Now I saw how she truly looked. I quelled my alarm.

As if reading my thoughts, she said, "My disease, my allergy to light, allows me only to live in the dark. My ears and eyes are designed to allow me extra-sensitive hearing and vision."

Yes, pupils enlarged to allow in more light when needed and shrunk in bright light to allow in less. The shape of her ears must work similarly to allow her to hear better. I'd never heard of such a disease. A wave of sadness clutched my innards and I wanted to do everything I could for her. It wasn't right that she live in the rank underground and slept on a dirt floor instead of living inside a house.

The sadness only grew stronger and I knew it was hers mingled with my own feelings. "Stay in my room. My parents won't know. My closet is large and the sun won't harm you." I almost didn't believe the words coming from my mouth. Of course my parents would know. How could I hide a person? Even though the house was large, my mom knew every inch.

"Thank you, but I can't do that. We would surely get caught. My home is underground and I need to return." Her words so profound, as if she'd thought the scenario before, or maybe she was reading my mind.

chapter 6

We walked and, for the first time, I noted her clothing. I guessed I was so taken aback with her beauty the first time we met and her true appearance this time that I hadn't set eyes on the rest of her. The lacy collar of the nightgown rested just below her neckline and full sleeves covered her arms. White showed in splotches around the dirt.

"Wait here," I said by the foot of the stairs.

She stopped, her head down, face staring at the grooves in the wood floor. I scurried up the stairs, considering whether I should bring her something to wear of mine or my mother's. Not willing to take the chance my mom would miss it, I opted for my room. In the back of my closet were clothes that no longer fit me, but she was smaller. Grabbing a shirt and pants, I scrambled back down the stairs.

Rabina wasn't where I left her. "Rabina," I called as I searched for her. Remembering she first contacted me through my head. I closed my eyes and listened, repeating her name in my head.

"Isandro," she responded.

Where are you? I thought.

"Right beside you," she answered, her chilly hand touching mine.

I popped my eyes open and folded my hand around hers. "Where did you go?"

Her head moved in the direction of my father's open study. Her eyes completely black, it was hard to tell if that's what they were seeing, although her words confirmed it. "Home."

"Take these," I pushed my clothes towards her chest. It was the gentleman thing to do, something my parents had always taught me.

She took them without a word and we walked through the corridor to her dark, dank lair.

When we returned to her sour-odored room I caught a slight whiff of another smell. It was metallic in nature like... my hand smelled the other night when I sucked my scratch -- blood. It smelled of blood.

"Thank you," she said and I felt the sincerity in her words as if no one had ever been so kind.

It was no sooner that I returned to my room then my parents came home. I curled on my side away from the door in case they checked on me. My mind sorting through the things I hadn't understood the past couple days -- magic and a girl with a disease to sunlight that allowed her amplified senses.

I'd nearly forgotten my parents' argument over my twelfth birthday. The focus whether I was ready or not, my mother holding steadfast that I wasn't. *Was this magic world what they were arguing about?* I rolled the idea around in my head and considered telling them the recent events, then decided against it. Papa would be upset about my sneaking out and I'd probably get a lashing. Mom would agree that I had disobeyed. I kept my mouth shut.

On Monday when we returned to school, Lawrence and Arthur dished out dirty glares, overcome with hate for me and Clara. It wasn't their disgruntled faces that told me how they felt, but a sensation. The night they attacked us in the woods I pushed their strong emotions out of me and Arthur had doubled over in pain. *Had I actually done that?*

The question plagued me, but also scared me. It wasn't in my vocabulary of the world to believe that was even possible. It didn't stop me, though, from avoiding Clara. Her blue eyes sad when I'd see her and turn the other direction, always walking away from her. As much as I evaded her, I was the opposite with Rabina. Every chance afforded to me I snuck into the brick corridor and to her underground room.

I never acclimated to the odor. As much as I tried, it was disturbing. Nevertheless, I couldn't leave her down there with no companionship. I shook my hands and dropped the metal jacks watching as they scattered against the ground. She bounced the ball and scooped up a jack. Her reflexes were quicker than mine. Maybe something to do with her disease.

"Tell me about the world above?" she asked.

She asked that question every time I saw her. I took my turn bouncing the ball and scooping up jacks. "It's beautiful. There are green trees and plants and flowers. The sky is blue; when there's no clouds the sun warms my skin. Not far from here is the bay. It leads to the ocean and its sandy shores."

She smiled. "I remember a little, like the birds in the air and the scent of flowers in bloom."

"What happened to your parents?" I'd never asked the question and hoped it didn't make me seem insensitive, but I couldn't help wondering. It seemed they must have abandoned her when the effects of her disease started to show.

She nodded her head and shrugged her shoulders. "I don't know." She paused, my emotions reading hers. She couldn't lie to me if she tried. "All I remember is waking up here, dawn's light streaming above me then the Earth shook, sealing the hole and my fate."

She'd never revealed that much and there was a hint of something absent and ambiguous in her words but I didn't feel it in her soul. I'd never exposed my "gift" to her. I'd come to think of it that way. My extra sense that allowed me to understand and feel what others felt. I didn't want her to feel vulnerable, although maybe that was one-sided since I knew of her extreme senses due to her illness.

"I'd like to take you above at night so you can breathe the fresh air and see the beauty of the foliage," I offered, fully expecting her to shut me down.

Instead, she raised her head. "I would like that."

"Tomorrow then." I smiled and bounced the ball, scooping up a handful of jacks from the solid dirt floor.

She returned my smile and for a brief moment I saw color in her eyes. A royal blue. But the moment was so quick it was probably nothing more than my imagination.

The following night, while my parents were sound asleep, I made my usual trip to see Rabina. My heart beat quickened as tonight I would take her above ground. If my parents caught me I'd be in more trouble than I'd ever faced, but the lashings I might receive didn't outweigh my concern for her. I couldn't place my finger on why I cared so much for her. Maybe it was that she lived below ground, maybe it was that she had no family, or maybe it was that I was falling for this odd-looking girl with a strange disease.

As her door clanked open I felt the excitement and fear inside her. She was unsure of what we were about to do but anxious to see the world outside the rank underground lair she lived in. Her footsteps were quieter than mine as we moved through the house to the back door. It was as if she knew every place the floor would creak and groan before she took a step.

I paused before opening the door, one hand rested on the knob. I clutched her hand with my free one. Its coolness no longer a shock to me. "Are you ready?"

"Yes." I felt her excitement but it wasn't the same as mine. For me it was the taboo and the idea I was pushing the line set by my parents. For her it was something more sinister, a wave of darkness pushed through her. I felt all of it and swore I felt the need for a solid heartbeat, blood pushing through veins. That was ludicrous. I had to have read that wrong.

Clutching her hand, we walked into the night. Her black eyes didn't change to allow in the moonlight. The moon a full round sphere glowing a bright yellow, stars dotting the dark, clear sky. She didn't appear to take notice until I mentioned it to her. Her eyes stayed a solid black and I swore they darted. How I could tell, I wasn't sure. It was more a feeling that she was... hunting.

She wiggled her hand free and, with a speed quicker than anything I'd ever witnessed, moved to a bush several feet from us and plucked a sleeping bunny from beneath it. Her movements were a flash in a few seconds' time. I hadn't realized what happened until I spotted the bunny in her hand and without wasting another second brought it to her mouth.

I hadn't wanted to believe it but my senses were correct. She was hunting and the bunny became her dinner. Horrified, I ran to her in an attempt to save the furry animal's life but I was too late. It was dead by the time I reached her, as if she'd sucked the life out of it.

Its little corpse limp in her hand, blood dripping from her mouth. "You can't do that," sputtered from my mouth. There were many other things that came to mind later but at that moment all I thought about was the poor bunny and how my friend was responsible for its cold-blooded death.

She dropped the animal; its little body hitting the ground sent a cringe into mine. Rabina ran the back of her hand over her lips, wiping the blood onto it. "The food you bring me is good but it doesn't fill me up. I need fresh food with a heartbeat." Her words came out shaky and unsure, as if I'd judge her for them.

I took a step backwards away from her. "You only wanted to come here and feast, not see the moon and stars."

"I'm sorry, Isandro. Don't hate me. In order to survive I need blood, fresh and warm." Her throat moved as she swallowed what I hoped was not a lingering drop of the poor animal's blood. "Is it part of your disease?"

She nodded. "I think so, but all I've had to eat for many years is rodents. I hear their heartbeat, feel the blood pushing through them, and I can't control it."

I stepped back again. "But you don't feel that about me?"

Her dark eyes met mine. "I do, but you're different. I can control it around you if..." the words hung in the air between us, "I have enough to eat before seeing you."

What did that mean? Did I need to keep bringing her up here to hunt? Was she running low on rodents? Or had her appetite increased since meeting me because she needed to quench her blood lust before I made my nightly trip to her underground room?

It was no wonder I smelled the metallic odor of blood and the stench of death. Her lair was swathed in it and it probably smelled good to her. I swallowed the bile rising in my throat. "I think it's time to walk you back."

She lowered her head as if ashamed. The action broke my heart. I felt her shame working its way through my bones. She was being honest. It wasn't her fault. She couldn't help her disease any more than I could help being healthy and unplagued by such a devastating illness. I repressed my fear and held out my hand for her to take.

She didn't act on it right away. After a few moments of silence and my out-stretched hand, she placed hers around mine and we walked back into the house.

I gently closed and locked the door behind us without making a sound. The house was so quiet that footsteps upstairs blasted my ears as if someone was stomping. "Isandro," came my father's loud voice, "Is that you?"

The steps creaked with his weight. I turned to Rabina and pointed to the stairwell leading to the attic. "Hide there until he's gone."

Without a sound and with super-human speed she fled up the steps and melted into the dark stairwell.

"Yes, Papa. I'm getting a glass of water." I hoped he didn't hear or sense the anxiety in my voice.

The steps halted on the stairwell. "Get to bed, son. School comes early in the morning." His footsteps retreated and I let out a breath, releasing my pent-up anxiety.

"Yes, Papa," I called.

Rabina had moved to the bottom of the stairwell and waited. I ushered her to my father's study, not worried about him hearing my footsteps this time and hers didn't make a sound.

chapter 7

I knew I couldn't avoid her forever, so when Clara cornered me after school it wasn't a shock. I'd evaded her long enough and, like Rabina, what she was wasn't her fault.

The sun glinted off her blonde hair with a golden halo and her lips didn't curl into a beautiful smile but made a straight line. Concern radiating from within her. "We need to talk."

"I know," I answered in shame. It was easier to face Rabina and the darkness than Clara who shone brighter than the sun. It was an avoidance tactic. I didn't want to accept what I might be. What might be inside me and, worse, what might be inside my father.

I almost showed Lawrence and Arthur my father's sword and would have if I had found it. Lawrence accused Clara and me of being children of Slayers. I didn't know what a Slayer was but figured

the sword was tied to it. The Slayer
meant to slay and slaying is usually done
with a weapon. A sword fit that bill. I
knew that instinctively now, although I
didn't the day we snuck into my father's
office. Whatever was inside me was
deeper than me and Clara.

"We can't do it here, someone
might overhear us."

I followed her willingly, listening
to the emotions within her. She was
scared but what of wasn't clear to me.
She was also worried for me and
brimming with the need to release the
emotions weighing heavily on her heart.

"What has you so tired in
school?" she asked.

"I haven't been sleeping well.
That's all." The lie came out with a crack
in my voice. I hoped she didn't catch it.

Reading her, I didn't sense that
she did, but her 'hmmm' told another
story. *Was it possible she could block things
from me?*

Keeping pace with Clara, my
mind continued thinking about Rabina.

She was the reason I succumbed easily today to Clara. What I'd witnessed Rabina do last night haunted me, yet all I could think about was how I would get her live food. I hadn't even seen the bunny she plucked from the ground. I lacked her inhuman speed and agility. Tracking above ground nightly might be too much, but she needed to eat.

I hadn't known that the food I brought her wasn't satisfying and I couldn't lie to myself. The idea she desired my blood made me nervous. It wasn't her fault but I didn't want her hunger unsated because I didn't want to become her meal. The worst part was that she frightened me less than the *magic* had.

"We're here," Clara proclaimed as she marched up the steps of a house on Desoto. It was every bit as large and intimidating as the one I lived in. A narrow door and four large windows made up the first floor. The last window sat at an angle where the porch moved out in a half circle around it, creating a wide berth. Three windows made up the second floor and two long windows with a balcony of sorts displayed on the third floor or attic. I couldn't be sure from my angle but the attic windows might be doors.

I followed Clara up the steps. The roof came up in a triangle above our heads. Instead of proceeding to the narrow front door she walked around the porch to the right. Set back several feet was another door with a balcony and another door on the second floor. I wanted to ask where we were but I had a good idea already. I sensed the buzzing in the air and its hum filled me up.

This was the witches' house. When his words soared into my head, it only confirmed my thoughts. *Come in.*

Clara opened the door and without hesitation strolled inside. His words flowing into my head felt different to when Rabina's had. Hers were more a straight jarring path but his seemed to follow different paths, as if lingering in my mind searching for something. They were warm like a fresh spring day. I shoved my thoughts of Rabina to my subconscious. If the man could speak into my head it wasn't impossible to think he could read what was in my head too. I wasn't sure I wanted him, or anyone, to know about her. My instincts told me it could be trouble for her if anyone at all found out.

Glossy woodwork framed the ceilings and floors. I didn't see the man but felt his presence as Clara took a step on the stairs ahead of us. They glowed in the same wood, along with the banister and molding on the wall. Natural light flooded through the windows, dousing the house. My mind turned to Rabina who would never enjoy such beauty. I quickly diverted the thought to avoid any possible mind reading that might be happening.

The stairway curved open to a large, airy room. A waist-high chest rested against the wall with an intricate flowery design painted on the front sliding doors. Two matching wood-framed chairs with plush red velvet cushions sat across from a matching couch. The thin legs didn't appear wide enough to hold weight but undoubtedly they were solid.

The witch sat with his long legs at an angle to his body. In the light I saw him clearly. His unusually long raven black hair styled in something one might expect for a pirate or someone without access to hair scissors and a razor. Only his was clean and clearly worn that way on purpose.

He raised his sharp chin enough to meet our gazes. "Sit please."

Clara sat before the words fully came out of his mouth. I took a moment then sat on the chair beside her, opposite him.

His soft brown eyes drifted to me and met mine. "I'm Mark. I understand this is all very new to you and that you are skeptical. I was too at first." His words evenly paced and rhythmic. "You are both light witches. This is something you are born with and means one of your parents is also a light witch. It's important you determine which one without alerting the other. We have hidden ourselves in society for thousands of years. Non-witches must not know we exist."

This was irrational and bizarre. My parents were normal people. I'd never seen glowing light balls sitting atop their outstretched palms or had their words filter into my head. Neither had ever done anything strange and out of the ordinary. "How can we tell?"

"Grab Clara's hand." Clara and I met glances as we took hands. "What do you feel?"

"Her hand?" I knew that wasn't the response he was looking for but I couldn't yet admit that I felt a buzz, a surge of something pass through me.

He didn't speak in words but his expression spoke for him; lowered brows and straight lips.

I licked my lip and answered sheepishly, "I feel a buzz."

His face remained solemn. "That is the sign you are light witches. You will feel a similar buzz from your witch parent. In the meantime, I can start your training. Clara has already begun."

She squeezed my hand as if to confirm it was OK to trust this man who claimed to be a witch. But I didn't trust him and was cynical. "Why? For what reason do I need to learn to use magic?"

That's when his lips parted and a smile crossed his face. "Because if you don't you can't defend yourself against the night magic. If you had never come into your powers you wouldn't be a threat to them, but you have and have used them. That imprint of magic can be felt by them and they will seek you out to destroy you."

"But why?" I stumbled over those two little words. Why would a witch have any reason to destroy me? I wasn't understanding.

"They work for the sorceress, doing her dirty work. Our purpose is to stop them."

As if Clara saw my puzzled expression she said, "They protect the evil in the world and we protect the good." Her words made more sense than his.

My layers of disbelief were slowly ebbing away. I wanted to believe Clara and I trusted her. "What can my magic do?"

She spoke instead of him. "Different things. We don't all have the same magic." The centerpiece on the table rose and hovered over the surface. "I have telekinetic powers." She lowered the centerpiece then curled her hand into a ball. As she uncurled it a small light glowed in her palm and grew. "You can do this too. All light witches have this ability."

I glanced at my hands, turning them over. I couldn't imagine making light and holding it. "Does it hurt?"

A synchronous chuckle escaped Clara's and Mark's mouths. "No, not at all," Clara said when her chuckle dispersed.

"So what else can my magic do?"

Mark's eyes widened. "I think you are an empath. They aren't common. It's a rather unique magic but can be just as dangerous, if not more so, to night witches because you can cripple them with their own sour minds and hearts."

Now it was my turn to widen my eyes in shock. I had thrown Arthur's hate and emotion back on him. I was responsible for dropping him to his knees. The revelation left my mouth hung open in an attempt to find the words that had disappeared.

Mark's triangle face squared as he spoke. "You already knew that. My abilities are telepathy and teleportation."

Words finally found their way out, although strangled. "Telepor-what?"

"Teleportation. He can go anywhere simply by picturing it." Clara's words were far too excited for me in that moment.

Mark ran his hands over his long legs. "But I have limits. I can't teleport to, say, France in one trip. That would take a couple trips and stopping in the Atlantic isn't a good option." A smile tugged at the corners of his lips as he stood, revealing his well over six foot height. "Take my hand both of you."

The command in his voice forced me to take action. I jumped off the chair and grabbed his outstretched hand. Clara did the same. If felt more like mind control, maybe that was his telepathy and the reason he could speak into our heads.

A hot, white light enveloped us and when it dissipated we were standing ankle-high in the ocean, the surf crashing over our shoes. The next second the light reappeared dropping us high on a mountain then a field then a city alley and finally back into the house on Desoto.

My words again left me, as what happened was impossible.

"It's not impossible, it's the magic I was born with," he said, responding to the words in my head.

"You read my mind!" It was an invasion. I was glad I'd pushed thoughts of Rabina out of my head. The second she

entered my mind I pushed her out again and focused on my parents. I'd never felt a buzz from either, so which was the witch? "How come you have two powers? Do all of us have two?"

"No. It depends on your lineage. In my ancestry, a telepath married a teleporter and so I have two magics. My power of telepathy is stronger than my power of teleportation," Mark responded, his words making a strange kind of sense.

"So one of my parents is an empath?"

He clasped his hands together as he sat back down on the velvet loveseat. "A strong empath." The undertones in his words told me he knew more than he was saying, or maybe it was my empathy...

I'd never felt a buzz from either of my parents. *Was it something that happened at a certain age?* I thought again of my parents' argument. My mother adamant that I wasn't ready, my father insisting I was. *Were they arguing over magic?* If so, one had broken a rule and let the other know of their abilities or maybe... maybe they were both witches. It was preposterous. I'd never felt a buzz, not even a slight tingle, from either.

As I reached my house I spotted the familiar, lanky form of Lawrence resting against a tree shading my neighbor's house. He didn't say anything but I felt his eyes on my back as I took a step towards the front porch. Wind hit my back carrying a message: *Get the sword.* I shuddered.

chapter 8

Lawrence's persistence with the sword made my mind reel as I ate my dinner. *What was so special about it? Was it magic? Did it have some type of light witch magic that if stolen by night witches they could control?*

"How are your studies?" my father asked in a tone I understood to know had a double meaning.

"They're good, Papa."

He sawed a knife across his slice of pork. Then pricked it with a fork and rested his hand on the side of his plate. "Is that so? I ran into your teacher who says you have trouble staying awake in class lately."

A profound statement. I fought the reaction to drop my eyes in shame. It was expected of me to finish out school and continue my studies. That's what males from affluent families did. "I've had trouble sleeping the past couple weeks. I'll do better."

"Why didn't you say something? A bit of warm milk and honey will get you right to sleep." My mother pushed her chair out and immediately went to mixing the concoction. Her back to me, I couldn't see exactly what she was doing.

"You are becoming a man, coming of age." My father glanced sideways at my mother. The message wasn't meant for me but her.

She set the milk on the table, avoiding eye contact with my father. The tension between them so strong it made the room stuffy.

I picked up the glass, "Thank you," and sipped. My birthday was seven days away. Maybe I didn't need to find out which one had magic, possibly they would tell me then. I finished the glass and excused myself, saying I was going straight to bed.

I woke in the morning, sun streaming through the curtain and bolted upright. I hadn't visited Rabina. My mom put something in the milk that made me sleep like a baby, unable to keep my eyes open. *She was the witch!* It was some potion she made. *Mark hadn't said anything about magic potions; was it possible?* It had to be.

The remainder of the week I allowed my parents to think I was drinking the warm milk and honey as I took it to my bedroom each night, tossing the potion out the window and leaving the empty glass on my nightstand. When I heard my father's snores I snuck down to his office and, taking a big risk, brought Rabina to ground level to hunt.

After school I met Clara and Mark. He showed me how to form a light ball in my hand and taught us control over it. "Feel the buzz inside you and imagine it in your hand," Mark coached.

It worked as I stared at the light buzzing in my palm. It was small at first but I learned to make it grow. He taught us control over our other powers, making me suddenly realize I was an empath which meant one of my parents, as Mark had said, was an empath too. It only came as a shock because if I could read emotions so could my parent, but neither had displayed it. If they could read me they'd know about Rabina, yet they slept soundly every night.

"Is it possible to have a different power than your parent?" I asked.

Mark raised a brow and I felt his mind push into my own. It was subtle and that's why I hadn't noticed when he first did it but now that I was learning control over my magic I understood what he was doing.

"Impressive," he said, avoiding my question.

"I felt you there."

"Just because they don't use the ability doesn't mean it's not there. Maybe they never used it and don't know they have it. Some witches never develop their power." He placed a palm against my light ball and arched it like a bridge.

Clara joined our bridge of light spanning it in a third direction. "My father is the witch," she paused. "Or a warlock, right? That would be the proper term."

Mark chuckled. "That is what humans call us. We call each other witches of the light, male and female the same."

The night before my birthday and the revealing of my witch parent. The heat of the excitement kept me awake. I hadn't been down to see Rabina the previous night, playing it safe, but I desired to see her now. To spend the night nocturnal, like her.

When I entered the corridor I felt something different -- a penetrating blackness. Its claws dug deep into my soul as if attempting to pull it out of me. Daggers of pain brought me to my knees. Rabina's pain. She wasn't alone. Something was there with her.

I fought the darkness and pushed onto unsteady feet, retreating to my father's office. I needed the sword. I could use it as a bargaining chip or a weapon. I rifled through my fathers desk, finding a set of keys along with ink and paper. I closed the desk drawers, not caring how loud I was. All I could feel was relentless pain and a deep well of darkness.

I felt along the bookcases lining the walls finding a secret door below. Inside was a long metal box that was locked. Remembering the keys in my father's desk I retrieved them and, finding one small enough to fit the lock, opened the metal box.

An orange glow radiated from the orange stone in the hilt, causing the silver blade to have a slight golden hue. I pulled the sword out, closed the box and slid it back into its hidden home then proceeded, lugging it through the corridor.

It was so heavy I didn't know if I could use it properly, but I had to try. If something was there with her, something evil, I had to try.

The closer I got the more of Rabina's pain I felt. It wasn't only pain but hunger pangs like someone was dangling a beating heart in front of her while preventing her from getting to it.

Go back please, Isandro, Rabina's voice came into my head. She hadn't done that for a while, stirring the already bubbling tension I felt.

Hoping her telepathy worked like Mark's I responded *No, I can't do that.*

Rabina's pleas for me to leave stung my brain as I pulled the stone from the wall and her door opened. I couldn't get past how someone else could be in the room with her. I always walked her back and locked the door. As impossible as it seemed, nothing was impossible. The last few weeks had taught me that.

The sword's hilt heavy in my hands, I maneuvered inside the dark room using its light to scan the area until I found Rabina's face. Her eyes widened as they took me in. Behind her stood a monster. Its claws surrounded Rabina's chest and fangs protruded from its mouth.

Something furry brushed past my leg. The light from the sword illuminated the animal enough for me to see the fluffy black and gray ringed tail of a raccoon scuttle into the hall. I turned back in time to see Rabina pounce at me, sinking her teeth into my neck as she pushed me backwards, like a wild animal, into the wall. I thrust the sword with both hands. It was an instinct. The blade ripped across Rabina's neck. She dropped to the ground and I plunged it through her heart, forgetting how weighty the sword was. The motion felt natural. Tears rolled over my cheeks. The sword plunked to the dirt as my hands released it.

A maniacal laugh erupted from the monster as something stung the opposite side of my neck from Rabina's bite. I sucked in all its emotional darkness; fear and sorrow filled me full, and I pushed it out into the creature. It flew backwards and crumpled to the floor, surrounded in its own misery.

A heavy wind rushed across the room, knocking me to my knees.

"You finally found it. Very good." Lawrence walked out from a dark, shadowy corner and leaned over, grasping the hilt of the sword. *How had I missed him and how did he get here?* I concentrated all my light and formed a buzzing ball in each hand then let them go. One sailed towards the monster, the other Lawrence, before I even considered what I was doing. It was an impulse.

Two more light balls whizzed past me, humming in my ears, catching my own balls of light and forming a super ball like a cannon it exploded, sinking deep inside the monster and Lawrence. It cooked them from the inside out. The monster becoming a pile of ash and Lawrence knocked backwards to his butt. My father's sword loosened from his hands. It turned on its own and plunged into his heart. The golden light from its hilt illuminating black blood as it soaked his shirt.

"Isandro," my mother's voice wailed into my ear and arms wrapped around me, electricity buzzing through me.

"Mom?"

She twirled me around and placed her hands on my cheeks. Her eyes searching mine, drifting to my neck. "Blood. You've been bitten. Come."

She called my father as she draped an arm around me and guided me out of the room. His large footfalls pounded in my ear louder than normal and I suddenly became weightless as I dropped to the ground. *She is the witch,* was my final thought as I passed out.

chapter 9

I woke on my bed, alone in my room. My parents' voices and an unfamiliar female voice were loud and clear as if they were standing beside me.

"There's nothing I can do. I'm sorry. I wish I could, but there is no cure for a Bloodseeker bite. You know that and we cannot change this. The moment he drinks human blood he will become one of them," said the unfamiliar voice.

"But he's a light witch. I saw it. He killed those Bloodseekers. He killed them. How could he do that if there is no cure?" said my mother, her voice shaky from crying yet firm in anger. I was numb to her pain. I could no longer feel it. Gazing at my hands I attempted to force the light into my palms but I couldn't find it. The spark was absent.

The unknown female responded, "But he's not a Slayer. They are the only light witches truly exempt from

Bloodseeker bites and only after they bond with their amulet."

The words and names foreign to me. The Slayer word came up again. *What was a Slayer?* My mother called Rabina and the monster Bloodseekers. *Is that what they were? Is that why Rabina needed blood? Fresh blood from animals?* My heart broke in two when I remembered the pain and desperation when Rabina sunk her teeth into me. Tears welled in the corners of my eyes and my nose stuffed up when I remembered I'd killed her with my father's sword.

What she was wasn't her fault. I replayed it through my head, the conversations between the adults moving to the background as I considered every option and what I could have done differently instead of killing her.

My father's loud voice cut in between the arguing females. It sliced through their words, shutting each up. "My son will not become a Bloodseeker! I won't allow it. He will drink the blood of animals." He stomped towards my room, each step so loud it brought pain to my ears as if they were on fire.

My door opened with a gentle hand, not what I expected of my father, but his bulky form told me it was him. His eyes rested on mine and he combed my hair back. "My son. You are awake." He wrapped his thick arms around my back and lifted me up, holding me tight against his chest.

Thump, thump. I heard each beat of his heart. It grew louder with each pound. His blood moved through his veins and arteries with a hiss. Crimson desires washed through my mind as I grasped what was left of my humanity, yelling in my head at my father, *No, papa. I don't want to do this. Kill me, papa.*

He let me go and I wiggled backwards, cupping my hands around my legs.

He called my mom. Her light steps sounded against the wooden stairs. "Keep him here. Don't allow him to move. He is ready to feed."

Did he hear me? How was that possible unless he, too, was a witch?

She raised her hand and gave it a twist, tears streaming down her face. A force wrapped around me, suspending me in place. I couldn't wiggle a toe, much less get out of bed. My mom was telekinetic like Clara. I tried to think of any time she used the magic before tonight and couldn't. I'd never seen it.

If telepathy worked on my father I hoped it would work on my mom. *Tell me everything please. Keep my mind from this hunger.*

Through sniffles she began. "Your father is the agate Slayer and empath. I'm a telekinetic light witch. Centuries ago an evil sorceress created the monsters you killed downstairs. They are named Bloodseekers because of their thirst for blood. Seven light witches came together and spelled seven amulets, each a different stone and color of visible light -- the Slayers. Each is from a light witch bloodline." She broke down in tears. I did my best to soothe her but my mind was slipping as I craved her blood more and more with each beat of her heart. My father was right to have her hold me in position and her telekinetic grip never let up as she finished the story.

I lost my light witch powers that day but never succumbed to the bloodlust. At first, my father kept me full on fresh animal blood. When he realized it satiated me he started to let me hunt on my own. I came and went from the tunnel and he designed another that went straight to my bedroom. Eventually we built interconnecting tunnels.

My parents buried me in a proper funeral. They are the only two people who know I still exist. It is night when I sit outside Clara's window and watch her sleep. She is my heart's desire but one I can never fulfill. She can't know I exist. She also is directly related to a Slayer -- the beryl telekinetic Slayer.

The Begotten is the name I use for what I am. Rabina was the first until she made me. Now I scour the city at night searching for others like me, saving them from turning into bloodsucking, heartless monsters. We feast on animal blood, but never on humans. It is the only way we can keep any part of our humanity.

Alarico

hidden journals vol.2

prologue

The year 1142, I shall never forget it. 'Twas the day of my rebirth. I was seventeen and a strong, healthy young man who was quick on my feet. I shrugged my shoulders and thought, *I'm too fast, nothing will happen to me.* Like children today I never thought it would... until it did.

A raven-haired vixen with ruby lips spoke to me, pulled me from my slumber. She was like Snow White, only her intentions were anything but pure. Like a pet I ran to her, conforming to her will, against my own.

It was late August, the breeze raised the sheer white curtains from the windows, candlelight bounced off the walls. In a silken bed she lay and, like the healthy teen boy that I was, I went to her.

She seduced me. No, she forced my will. Any part of me that wanted to fight her was handcuffed metaphorically.

One bite from her succulent ruby lips subdued me and the next drained me. She offered my flail blood-let body a chalice of thick red liquid. A potion to make me the first. I craved the metallic red fuel that gives my veins life -- blood.

This night I accept my orders from our Crimson Queen. I've been chosen to accompany the night witches into the village.

Whispers through the darkness and quiet, knowing glances, tell us something is afoot. An event that will change the status of power.

For centuries we have ruled with no consequence. The humans causing havoc and pillaging more villages than us, all in the name of religion, but that may come to an abrupt end. The powers are shifting. I feel it, she feels it.

She has gifted us with compulsion, telepathy, immortality, and extreme speed. But with any gift comes a curse. We can't survive in the daylight, and remember little of our lives before the thirst.

I say this only to myself, but our job is one of the lowest standards. She gave us all these precious gifts but the worst part of our curse is we fuel her. The blood we drink drives her immortality. Anything that powers her powers us and gives us life. Therefore, we are at her mercy.

We have no will of our own. Through the blood that fuels us she speaks into our minds. No matter the distance, we can't run from her.

I am a Bloodseeker. We are Bloodseekers. Our thirst fuels the pyramid that gives what she created life.

chapter 1

"**S**he said you were young but you are a mere child," chided the night witch. His long, dark mop tied back in a ponytail.

You will feast on my call, not before, I brain messaged my disciples waiting in the woods surrounding the village. Disdain seeping from the night witch's eyes. I wanted them to feast on him but I knew the rules.

Without responding to his snide remark I replied, "Shall we go? Time is of the essence."

He pulled his horse around. "I didn't bring an extra."

"I prefer to walk." My legs could carry me quicker than a horse. It was one of my gifts. The night witches saw me as any other Bloodseeker, not for what I truly was.

The torches' light grew brighter as we headed down the mountain. Leaving the horses tied to trees outside the village we walked in from various directions. Finding the tavern, I pushed the door wide, letting myself in.

The humans inside becoming throbbing veins and arteries calling for me. I also had the gift of self-control -- something my disciples weren't born with. It was a skill. I felt their restlessness outside the village as they also smelled the feast inside the walls.

I sipped my beer, setting the mug on the clumsy table as it unsteadily shifted beneath the force. My ears listening to the conversations, none causing any alarm. Mere humans who called themselves Christians, yet filled their nights with debauchery. In my opinion we did them a favor.

A sweet scent drifted through the smelly, unbathed men, causing me to search the room for its source. In the corner, under a hooded cloak that did little to hide her femininity. Chestnut locks crossed her porcelain cheeks. Her green eyes met mine, and for a second our gazes locked until she glanced away. No doubt I'd made her afraid.

She didn't belong here. It wasn't a place for a young woman of her stature. Her mind became my playground as I gently eased my way into her thoughts, curious why she was in such a place. Finding her mind a tough place to impose my own, I lifted my mug and joined her.

Green eyes filled with fear widened as I drew closer. Her hand lowered to her waist as if grabbing for a knife. I chuckled inwardly. As if a mere blade could harm me. But I admired her instinct, her moxie.

Reaching her table, I pulled out the chair opposite her. "I can't help but ask why such a beautiful young maiden is hiding in a tavern," I said in a low tone barely above a whisper.

Her lips pinched as if expelling any words would bring her discomfort. She then cleared her throat and in a deep, low voice attempting to hide that she was a female replied, "You know not what of you speak."

The sweet scent poured from her lips, it was no doubt her. "Whatever you are hiding from I can help you." *Yes, I could give her something else, a place as one of my disciples.*

"There is nothing you can do for me except walk away and forget you met me." She didn't attempt to hide her voice. The tavern door swung shut and she stood, drawing her hood further over her face. "I must go now."

I glanced towards the door -- soldiers. They were no match for my skill set. I was curious, why was she hiding from them? Surely a young maiden of her stature wasn't on their wanted list. I stood. Cocking my head to catch her glance I whispered, "Stay behind me." I wasn't of formidable size but large enough to hide her small frame.

A scowl formed on her face as she relented and stayed behind me as we strode towards the door. The soldiers broke up, their eyes searching the tavern, obviously looking for someone. The chatter among the debauchers, who were moments earlier drinking and merry, suddenly changed to silence. Every floorboard creaked beneath our boots. Maybe leaving wasn't prudent, nonetheless, we were already on our way out and so continued our journey towards the door.

A staunch soldier, his shoulders broader than an ox's yoke, side-stepped in front of me, blocking the way. He pushed his hand against my chest. "Where do you think you're going?"

"The day was long and so it is time for rest," I replied in a soothing voice.

He glanced over my shoulder and pulled his sword then stepped beside me and pushed it against my back as if shoving me forward so he could glance the young maiden. "And who is this?" He brought the sword along her hood and eased it down but I caught his hand, twisted it until he dropped the sword then grabbed it in that moment, quicker than his human eyes could see, and thrust it into his chin.

All eyes were now on us. The residents sat breathless and ready to rumble. The soldiers drew their swords. I was hoping to avoid all this but wasn't left with a choice. The sword's point holding the chin of the soldier, I stated in careful words, my eyes drilling into their minds, "You will let us leave and not follow. You will continue your drinking and not remember any of this."

The soldiers put their swords away, the crowd continued their conversations and we slipped out the door.

"How did you do that?" she asked as I rushed her outside the village gates.

We slowed our pace. "It's a secret I will share with you, but not until you tell me why you are here?"

"I don't think that's any of your concern," she snapped.

"It is when someone saves your life."

"Thank you. I am grateful, but I must go." She pulled her cloak tight to fend off the night chill.

"No, it's not safe. You are staying with me."

Now, the village is yours, I mind messaged my disciples.

She huffed, "You aren't safe with me. They will come for you. Now I must go." She turned on her heel and halted when my disciples ran towards us, heading for the village gates. Their eyes heat seekers and they wouldn't spare her except I shielded her, wrapping my cloak around her.

Her body close to mine shuddered as they rushed past us, inside the walls, screams filling our ears as I slipped her over my shoulder and carried her away.

Her fear quickly subsided at her captivity. Her tiny palms pummeling my

back and her own screams for me to
release her louder than the dying
villagers'.

chapter 2

The Crimson Queen's words echoed in my mind as I carried the maiden up the mountain. Her breathing and heartbeat returning to normal, she stopped battling me. Her strength no match to mine. *You will know by the scent of their blood if they can be reborn or used as food.* It wasn't that simple, I'd learned. The ones who fought rebirth were bull-headed, they lacked the ability to discipline themselves, attempted to refuse orders, and often went rogue, but they had their place and so I didn't destroy them.

Those who were willing embraced their fate and were the disciples I kept the closest but they, like me, had made their own rogue creatures. I needed her to want, welcome, and desire to be reborn. I set her body against the cave wall. The hood of her cloak dropped, uncovering her face. She was beautiful, more so than I imagined hidden under her cloak. Soft porcelain skin encircled by chestnut curls that poured over her shoulders.

She folded her arms defiantly over her chest, her eyes focused on the wall behind me. Unlike my disciples I didn't only see heat but retained my human vision too. I wasn't sure the Crimson Queen was aware. There were other quirks about me that set me apart from them. I kept those to myself. It was the only advantage I had. "Now, why are you running?"

She continued her stare at the wall, her lips pursed tight. I had patience but not time. "OK, I'm Alarico but you may call me Lars."

"Caty."

It wasn't much, but it was a response. "You've traveled, been to other villages. What are they saying?"

"I don't know. I keep to myself."

"Yes, and that's how you know what's being muttered."

She dropped her arms to her sides, letting her palms fall against the cave floor. "The same ole stuff," she shrugged.

Under most other circumstances I'd believe her, except I heard a hint of deception in her tone. Before I could speak again, she said, "Why do you ask? Why do you care? You obviously don't belong to a village but are a nomad with your own agenda."

She was feisty. I changed the subject. "The soldiers were after you." I paused. "I kept you safe--"

She interrupted, "You have powers. You're a witch."

I chuckled. "No, I'm not a witch but I will share my secret after you share yours."

"You think me funny?" She raised her brows and took a deep breath. "I'm to marry an older man that I don't love. My father is... he's important and therefore so am I. Those soldiers weren't sent to kill me but retrieve me. Bring me back to a life sentence worse than death."

Nobility married nobility whether the match was wanted or not. Women didn't have the choice; their place was to obey men. "And is there a young man who you do love?"

She dropped her head. "No, but I want to make that decision and have the chance to find that love."

An idealistic young woman. If I had the capacity to love it was slowly falling for this insubordinate young lady with her devilishly delicious green eyes. I understood the lack of free will. My fate was sealed just as hers, only I couldn't run away from mine. "I'm sorry."

Her eyes softened, her fingers drawing circles in the dirt. "Have you been in love?"

"No. Now what have you heard in the villages?"

"What do you mean?"

As a human, she wouldn't be able to spot a light witch if it met her in an alley or served her a mug at a tavern, but it was worth a try. "Something quiet, something people speak of in private."

"How would I know? I've been living in alleys, hiding in barns," she snipped, taking the defensive again.

I reached into her mind again, this time not so gently. She scrunched her face and pressed her hands against her temples. "Get out of my head!"

She ejected me from her mind. Humans didn't do that. They were weak willed.

"I'll tell you!" she said, as if unaware she'd pushed me. "Just don't do that again."

"I spent the night sleeping under a hay bale in a barn, several people came, entered, unaware I was there and spoke. They talked about magic. They were witches! You see why I didn't want to tell you. Witches, and I didn't turn them in. Instead I snuck out in the morning before dawn."

"And what did these witches say?"

"They spoke in riddles about spelled stones and where the land met the sky in shades of pink and gold. I don't know what it meant and, like I said, I left before the sun came up." Her heartbeat kicked up a couple notches while she told the story. Her pulse raced beneath her skin.

"In your travels, did you see such a place?"

She nodded. "It's your turn."

I held up my hand for her to be quiet and mouthed, "There's someone outside."

I felt it more than I heard it. A rogue. Without complaint or defiance, she didn't move a muscle. I pulled my sword and walked towards the darkness leading further into the cave. Using my ears to see, a form, squat on all fours, humanoid, was lurking in a corner. "Stand, show yourself."

It scampered further into the tunnel. Smarter than it, I grabbed the girl. "We must leave here. It isn't safe for you. I'm quicker. Let me carry you."

She didn't argue, as if now realizing I saved her not only from the soldiers but the monsters -- my disciples.

Fear flashed in her eyes and her voice carried into my head: *Like those you cloaked me from.* But I wasn't sure the words came from her mind or if I imagined it. Sweeping her into my arms, I ran from the cave.

Serval rogues surrounded the exit. *Her blood smells delicious. You owe us a meal.*

I owe you nothing. I would have killed you if it wasn't for our Queen. You let us go now or you will die by my sword, your black hearts pulled beating from your bodies, spilling your thick, black blood as they turn to ash.

I placed her onto her feet and pushed her behind me. "Stay close, hold onto me." Her tiny body grabbed around my middle, her fingers enclosed around my chest. She understood the fear was real, her pulse racing again. I fought my own urges to taste her blood. Her type was erotic and satiating. That is what made them so desirable to rebirth. Their blood was equivalent to an orgasm.

Stifling my urges, I drew my sword. Taking deliberate steps, I walked past the rogues who moved out of our way. Their black eyes filled with desire, their claws extended and fangs bared, noses sniffing her honey blood. I felt their breath warm on my neck as they closed in.

My speed beyond theirs, I grabbed the closest one and sliced the blade of my sword across his neck. His head hit the ground with a thump, followed by his body, and rolled as I pulled his beating black heart from his chest. They stepped backwards out of my grasp. I squished his head between my fingers. Black blood dripped from my hand, puddling in the dirt.

I held the heart up in my hands until we were clear of them, then tossed it between the group and swept Caty into my arms as we disappeared into the night.

The Vampires Next Door

Prologue

St. Augustine, 1823

Cara shivered, the stone cold floor beneath her. Shrieks sliced through the air above her, echoing through the stone walls. A moldy stench, thick in the surrounding air, drifted up her nostrils. The temperature dropped several degrees as a breeze touched her head. She dared to open her eyes and stare into the darkness surrounding her, peeling one eye open and then the next.

"Cara," sounded a soft voice, almost a whisper. A warm touch caressed her hand, a shadowy figure flashed before her eyes. "You need to leave." The soothing voice didn't elicit fear but warmth and love. Her eyes searched for whom it belonged to. A breeze brushed against her and the voice whispered in her ear. "You need to go. I can lead you."

She tilted her head and gazed upon a transparent woman, no more than twenty. Her flaxen hair fell across her shoulders, circling her heart-shaped face. "Who are you?" Cara stammered.

"I'm Alda, once like you. They've been here for centuries, before the pirates, before the first settlement. The true first inhabitants of this continent."

"Who are they?"

"They are Bloodseekers. Come now!" The urgency in her voice resounded inside Cara. She jumped to her feet and followed the apparition. Alda's white bodice hugged her torso, the black hem grazing the stone floor.

Light from candles illuminated the darkness as they wound through a narrow passageway, as one candle lit ahead of them, the one behind went dark. The brightness of each light cast a glow on the shadow beside it, lighting the faces of each ghost. One apparition after another, men and women, blood drenching their shirts and bodices from the fang marks in their necks. The chilly air sent waves of shivers spiraling through Cara's body. She lifted her arm to touch a girl, no more than twelve, but her hand went through the child's face.

They came upon a fork in the passage, Alda motioned for her to stop. Quickening footsteps sounded from the right. "Plaster yourself against the wall, into the shadows. They see heat, our lack of it will protect you."

Cara did as asked. Not questioning Alda. She knew the footsteps belonged to a Bloodseeker. One had come into her home and killed her family, draining them of every drop of blood. She tried to escape, to run, but he was too quick. His dark eyes bored into hers. And a voice inside her head commanded her to stop. Her body froze in place. She tried to move but his mind controlled the core of her brain and she collapsed, waking up on the stone floor.

Her mind swarming back to the present, she pressed herself against the wall, the shadowy apparitions swarmed around her, blanketing her in darkness, shielding her from the Bloodseeker. His footsteps halted at the fork, as if deliberating which direction to go. He turned and followed the corridor leading to the room she'd left, he halted. His black eyes glowed through the shadows surrounding her. She closed her eyes tight, to avoid his mind commands and held her breath. Cara stayed as motionless as possible, controlling the tremors threatening to shake her body.

Her sense of hearing heightened with her eyes squeezed shut, she heard his footsteps walk away from her and continue through the corridor. She popped her eyes open and watched his form through the corner of her eye. When he disappeared around the corner, Alda motioned for her to follow. *He'd know she wasn't there. He'd look for her.* The apparitions parted as Cara moved away from the wall.

Alda floated up the stairwell as Cara followed with gentle footsteps, careful not to draw his attention. A wooden door appeared before Cara as she reached the top of the stairs. Alda motioned for her to open it, the hinges creaking as she pushed it.

Moonlight from the crescent moon streamed through the parted heavy curtains, bathing the room in enough light that Cara could see. Dozens of ghosts swarmed the room. Now, able to see them clearly, she gasped. Their skin tones and origins varied - black, white, and varying shades of brown. None older than her. Their styles of dress told her many lived centuries before her. A young black ghost hovered in front of her, clothed in a thick graying dress. Her gentle brown eyes sent a burst of warmth through Cara's quaking, goose-pimpled body.

Alda soared towards a bookshelf and pointed to a nondescript brown leather book. "Pull it."

Cara hurried towards the shelf and lifted the book, the shelf easing back to reveal another room.

"Take the book inside the room. The door will close behind you."

Cara didn't argue. Thundering sets of footsteps pounded the floor behind her, only moments from catching her she dived into the room. The book case closed, leaving behind all the ghosts except Alda. A Bloodseeker rushed towards it, catching it with his hand. He forced the heavy door open. Cara scooted away from his grasp.

A bright red light flickered from the corner of the dark room. "Grab the light!" Alda yelled. Cara scurried towards it, dropping the book as she reached for it. She held it firmly in her hand and tugged, but the object was caught on something she couldn't see in the dark.

The Bloodseeker dived for her, catching her other arm in his firm grasp. A blast of white light diffused through the room from the object Cara clutched in her hand. He pulled her towards him. She tightened her grasp as the object and the nail it was stuck on slackened from the wall. The Bloodseeker, too late to stop her, screamed in agony as the light blasted him against the door, his body engulfed in flames.

The light enveloped Cara, pushing its way through her body. She burst into fire, the flames licking the walls, then eddying into nothingness. Her ginger hair now crimson red, her amber eyes shining as garnets in the darkness. Beneath her skin, muscles exploded to the surface.

"What's happening?"

A smile widened on Alda's face. "You're the one. We've waited for you."

"What do you mean and how come I can see you and they can't?"

"You are a Slayer, that's why you see us. As long as you wear the amulet you will be indestructible and invisible to the Bloodseekers. They won't be able to harm you. Your job is to find others like yourself and slay every last Bloodseeker. Don't ever take it off and keep it protected beneath your clothes. Should it fall into their hands they will use it against you. You see us because you are special. All the answers are in the book.

Take it, place the amulet around your neck and leave now!"

Cara leaned over and grabbed the book. She then pulled the glowing amulet over her head. "What about you and the others?"

"You have freed us. We are forever grateful but you must leave."

Cara hurried towards the door, stepping on the Bloodseeker's ashes. The door opened for her and she ran through the house, ghosts guiding her way. She dodged the Bloodseekers, their dark glowing eyes searching, fangs sharp as daggers protruding from their upper gums. Their blood covered mouths saturated the air with the scent of iron. Claw-like fingers sliced through the air, scratching her clothes as she sprinted past them, hurdling tables and furniture with skill and agility unknown to her.

Finally, reaching the front entrance, she twisted the golden knob on the large, chunky door and ran into the morning's first light. Dawn. The sun rising just above the horizon. She stepped onto the porch, Bloodseekers on her trail. Stumbling down the steps, she landed face first in the dirt. Scrambling she lifted herself upright and quickly turned towards the house.

A tall, thin Bloodseeker hissed, shielding his face as he sank into the house, flames licking his hands. The sun's light rose bigger and brighter in the sky, immersing the house in radiance. The ground shook. She sprinted.

Reaching the relative safety of the tree line, she turned in time to watch the ground part around the house, swallowing it. Thousands of lights glowed as the ghosts swirled into the atmosphere, rising high into the sky as they disappeared. Screams reverberated in the air surrounding her as the Bloodseekers were burned and buried.

She cupped her ears and knelt, curling her head towards her knees to muffle their death screeches. Unable to stifle the noise, tears rose to her eyes from the pain in her throbbing ears. As soon as the screeching began, it stopped, and the earth filled in above the house. The ground appeared undisturbed. The sun shone high in the sky, erasing the dreadful night.

Cara lifted the amulet hanging against her chest, a large red stone set in the center surrounded by, and hanging on, a silver chain. She clutched it, the book tucked beneath her arm, and marched down the road. Not a soul peered outside their windows or took notice of the event.

The house was wiped from existence and erased from St. Augustine's inhabitants' minds. Cara's secret.

Chapter 1

Alison

Music surging from the apartment next door startled Alison awake. Her body rolled off the couch with a soft thump, landing on an assortment of throw pillows she'd kicked off during her nap. She pulled herself off the floor and rubbed the sleep from her eyes. Mouth dry as the Sahara, she headed towards the kitchen for water. A shrill female scream vibrated against her eardrums, causing her to jump and drop her empty tumbler. It crashed to the floor with a loud thunk, mimicked by the shattering glass outside her front door.

The apartment complex was always quiet, especially after dark. It had to be the new neighbors. After sunset, they'd moved into the adjoining apartment. As a lonely girl in a new city, she'd watched them with admiration. Two women, neither over the age of twenty-five, single women living on their own. One with long, brown wavy hair and eyes bluer than any she'd seen before. A surreal blue. The other girl had blonde highlights throughout the light brown hair, framing her flawless face and intense green eyes. Both had curves in the right places.

Self-conscious, she had compared her still developing body to their mature ones. Her gut swelled over her sweatpants and her chest had barely sprouted. She wore an A-cup to make herself feel better, but really she didn't think anyone noticed when she went braless. At the moment her admiration for them plummeted; beautiful or not, they were an annoyance!

Two voices, one female the other male, argued in the breezeway, the open air hallway between the apartments, upsetting her, but also piquing her natural teenage curiosity. She peered through the peephole hoping to catch sight of someone in the breezeway between the apartments but all she saw was the apartment across the hall. Her own front door blocking the view of the adjoining apartment.

"I hate you!" Then the door slammed so hard it made the walls tremble and the door shake. Alison's face pressed against the door, she yelped from the jolt against her nose. Rubbing it, she moved away and strolled back to the kitchen, picked up her tumbler and poured filtered water into it, drinking it all in several successive gulps. Catching her breath she considered her options. She could knock on their door and ask them nicely to lower their music or she could wait it out.

Home alone, as her mother worked as a nurse at Flagler hospital, and hundreds of miles from her father and best friend, she was unsure what to do, but didn't feel knocking on the door was the best choice. Actually, the idea freaked her out. Instead, she padded to the coffee table, picked up her tablet and checked the time. She was overly dismayed when her tablet screen displayed eleven p.m.

A tad scared but nosy and irritated, she slid the patio door open and listened, maybe they were wrapping up the party. All she heard was murmuring half-drowned by the music. Upset, lonely and slightly frightened she sent her BFF in Virginia a message: *I hate my life. New neighbors are crazy. I miss you.* She knew Vicky was asleep like normal people and wouldn't see her message for several more hours.

Alison laid her phone on the table and gazed towards the heavens. A chunk of moon peeked out from the surrounding clouds. Always interested in lunar phases as most paranormal books she read featured the moon was an important piece of the story, and each phase having a specific meaning. The most well-known were the werewolves who morphed during a full moon, but red moons and blue moons had meanings too. Her body shuddered as the party next door continued, but the steady purr of a familiar vehicle kept her plastered to the chair.

Within seconds an emerald green Charger hugged the road as it passed her screened patio. Her eyes moved with it as the driver swung around the curve. She jumped from the plastic patio chair, grabbed her phone, her heart beating fast within her chest, and with a sigh, stepped inside. Almost forgetting her troublesome new neighbors. She slid the heavy glass door closed, bolting all the locks and tugging to be sure.

She raced toward the dining room window and parted the blinds, a large breezeway with philodendrons planted in the middle separated the apartments. She recognized the emerald green Dodge Charger and its driver, Rodham. To her, his chiseled body screamed for every teenage girl in a fifty mile radius to pay attention. He lived kitty corner to her apartment and directly across the hall from the new, loud neighbors.

He rounded the corner of the building, keys jingling in his hands, eyes shooting a glance across the hall towards the partying neighbors' apartment. Well defined muscles on his forearm bulged as he twisted the key in the lock. She imagined herself wrapped in those arms, his full lips kissing her neck and drifting behind her ears. Still a virgin with no prospects or past boyfriends, thoughts of Rodham filled her waking and sleeping mind. Under no circumstances did she think a hot, dreamy creature like Rodham would date an ordinary, overweight, ginger like her because she lacked the talent and looks to suck men into her web. Rodham closed the door and her moment of teenage lust ended.

Dropping the blinds, she sauntered to the fridge and lifted the papers hung on the fridge with magnets, searching for an emergency number for the apartment complex. Her mother was organized, down to every detail. As the thought brushed through her mind, she glanced at the pillows still lying on the floor and made a mental note to pick them up before bed.

With a triumphant grin, she found the number and lifted it off the fridge.

Loud neighbors at eleven p.m. was an emergency in her book. She dialed the number and it directed her to leave a message. *What if I was dying? What if someone broke in and I was shivering in terror in my closet? Whatever*, she shrugged and left a message, tossed the pillows onto the couch and crawled into bed, drawing the comforter over her head, and sticking in her earbuds. She turned up the volume, attempting to drown the commotion next door and opened her tablet to her current book, *City by the Bay*.

Thirty minutes later a pounding on the front door interrupted her reading, and a shudder ran down her spine. She curled further under her covers like a frightened turtle inside its shell.

Rodham

A bottle cap skittered across the cement breezeway as Rodham rounded the corner. It landed in the dirt next to a philodendron leaf. A shattered glass bottle twinkled in the lights, its contents sprayed across the cement wall, puddling on the concrete beneath. The heavy beat from the music across the hall thumped against his eardrums.

When he drove past the apartment, he captured a glimpse of the new neighbors. Several people stood on the patio, each holding drinks in their hands. The sliding glass door open, he saw into their apartment, where a woman with blondish hair danced against a dark haired man. Her back rubbing his chest, she slid down him, her flowing hair trailing across his torso. Her partner leaned his face towards hers as she grabbed a handful of his dark hair.

Rodham fumbled with the lock, aware the apartment across the hall was empty when he'd left with his friend, Adrian, for Daytona to surf. Now, new, annoying neighbors partied and littered the breezeway. He wondered how the quiet ginger next door was faring against the noise. Always aloof with her tablet in front of her face - at the beach, the pool, slung in a hammock on the shore of the manmade lake at the apartment complex.

Her amber eyes mysterious and deep, ginger hair trailing her back with gentle waves falling across her shoulders, freckles kissed her porcelain cheeks. Intent on her tablet, she always twisted stray strands between her fingers. From the corner of his eye he caught her amber eyes peering from her parted blinds, biting her natural cherry colored bottom lip, watching as he hurried and closed the door, locking out the new, annoying neighbors.

One finger pushed against his ear, his cell phone meshed against his other, Rodham's father acknowledged he was home with a quick flash of his eyes, then he squinted and bent over talking to the person on the other end of the line.

His mom sat, feet propped on the coffee table and plugs in her ears. Her back against the soft cushion of the sectional. Closed captioning jogged across the TV screen. She waved at him as he disappeared into his room. Beach sand stuck to every part of his body, he gathered clean clothes and rushed into the shower.

He allowed the warm water to wash the sand down the drain, the cute ginger filling his thoughts. Fully focused on her, a set of dagger-tipped fangs interrupted his thoughts. A single drop of blood hung in the air as it fell from the point of a fang. A thunderous knock blasted him out of the vision. Catching the shower's side handle to keep from slipping, he knocked the back of his head against the tile wall, hard enough to give him a temporary headache. He scurried out of the shower, both his parents' were watching something through the parted blinds.

Chapter 2

Alison

Alison yanked the earbuds out of her ears and listened. The knocking stopped, the music stopped, and muffled voices drifted through the wall. Throwing off her covers, she hurried towards the dining room window, attempting to catch a glimpse. All she saw was the black-clothed, burly back of a police officer scolding her neighbors.

"We've had complaints. This is a residential area and we're going to have to ask you to keep your music down," the officer said in a deep voice.

Across the hall, Rodham's ebony face appeared through parted blinds. His sable eyes met her amber orbs locking them in a gaze. *He noticed me!* Thought Alison, the ambiguous girl whom he hadn't paid one ounce of attention to all summer. Warmth tingled through her body and she all but forgot about her matted bed-head, and Tinker Bell pajamas. The expanded-second locked gaze ended, and he dropped his blinds back in place.

She twirled her body away from the window and, in a dreamy state, leaned against the wall, thoughts of the day she followed him to the beach, flitted through her head. She'd poised her chair under an umbrella, sprayed SPF 130 over her entire pale body, placed a floppy hat on her head and watched him with stars in her eyes from behind the pages of her book while pretty girls with dream bodies in their bikinis flocked towards him like bees to honey. His brown skin velvet beneath the sun. She pushed her book, *Beyond the Hidden Sky*, over her face and read, catching glimpses of Rodham. In her one-piece with a baggy T-shirt to cover her jelly stomach she didn't think she compared to the other teens.

She peeled herself off the wall and strolled to her bedroom. *He noticed me!* Sinking into her bed she savored our moment in her mind, silence next door - she fell asleep.

Sun filtering through her window awoke her the following morning. She crept towards her mother's room, peeking around the corner of her opened door. She lay on her bed, burrito-wrapped inside the covers, feet poking out the end. Alison sighed relief that her mother was home. She'd grown used to her absence at night and had felt safe enough until last night.

Her stomach grumbling for food, she strolled into the kitchen, poured a bowl of cereal and ate while she turned on her tablet and continued reading her current book.

Hours later, her mother stretched her arms as she exited her bedroom and ambled into the kitchen. With a yawn she said, "Good afternoon, sweetie."

Peeling her eyes from her tablet and current fictional world, Alison acknowledged her mother from her prone position on the couch and lifted her eyes responding, "Hi, Mom. I fixed lunch, frozen lasagna and garlic bread."

"What did I ever do to get such a wonderful daughter?" She spied Alison's tablet. "I love all the reading you do. It helps the mind grow, but I hate seeing you inside all day, every day. That's why we bought you the car so you could get out, explore your new surroundings, meet new people. This is St. Augustine, the oldest city in the U.S., there's more than enough to keep you busy and entertained." She gently pushed Alison's legs towards the back cushion of the couch and sat, pecking her on the cheek.

Alison's parents had bought her a 2000 Corolla, not a bad first car. In fact, she thought it was an excellent first car - everything worked. The problem was they lived in Florida and she detested starting the car and setting the air conditioning to full blast for ten minutes before she could sit in it without melting or touch the steering wheel without second degree burns.

Her next problem was the friend issue. As an introverted book nerd, it took her years to build the relationships she had - Vicky, she was it. Her only friend. She anticipated she'd be spending the two years left of high school alone.

Alison's phone vibrated and she glanced at the message, Vicky responding to her late night text. *Miss you! Talk later, school shopping.* She wished she was in Virginia shopping with her, the way they'd done the past few years, since their parents deemed them old enough to wander the mall without 24/7 parental supervision.

"I miss Vicky, my high school, the mountains, the cooler night air."

Her mother sighed and brushed her hand through Alison's hair. "Honey, I know this is difficult for you. But your dad travels a lot. I was offered a job here. This is our home now. School starts next week, try and make friends."

"I know. I'll try." She bit her lower lip. "And when the weather gets cooler I'll explore the city." After her parents' divorce, her mother, who'd spent sixteen years as a stay at home mom, dusted off her nursing degree and sent her resume all over the U.S., hoping to land a job. She did, in St. Augustine, to Alison's bad fortune.

Her mother stood and wandered towards the kitchen, cutting a slice of lasagna and placing it on a plate, then sighed as she popped it in the microwave. "I've been working a lot, paying moving expenses. Once they're paid up we'll do more exploring together."

Facing away from her mother, Alison rolled her eyes and shrugged, the only exploring they'd done together was watching an IMAX movie at World Golf Village. And it was an excellent outing but, other than that, her mother constantly worked. Alison was old enough to understand child support didn't pay everything. She also understood her parents continued an amiable relationship if nothing else than for her, and her father would do more to help them out. Her mother, proud and stubborn, refused any money other than the court dictated amount.

She contemplated telling her mother about the neighbors but chose against it, assuming it was a one-night thing.

As soon as the sun went down, the neighbors' thumping music and partying began, growing louder as the night progressed. She built up the nerve to walk to her front door, replaying what she would say in her mind. As she turned the knob she chickened out, her anger inside recoiled and she stuck her earbuds in and read instead.

After midnight a thump hit her bedroom wall, she leaped off the couch in response. The decorative Asian fan above the couch shifted. Several more thumps followed, sounding like a body thrown against the wall. She stood in the doorway, expecting someone to burst through the wall any second. A shrill banshee scream shuddered through the air, piercing her eardrums, and vibrating through her head. In pain, Alison crumpled to the ground, holding her head between her hands.

Frozen in pain, she gripped the floor and dragged her body along it to the couch, reached her hand onto the cushion and fumbled for her phone. Then the noise stopped. Her fingers brushed against her phone and she snatched it up. Poised on the floor, she scrolled through her short phone log and redialed the emergency number then buried herself into the couch, encasing her fear-shivering body in a throw blanket.

www.ingramcontent.com/pod-product-compliance
Lightning Source LLC
Chambersburg PA
CBHW032035180726
48284CB00008B/2594